Japanese format, reading from right-to-left, to present the work as the creators originally intended.

Yeah, really sexy!

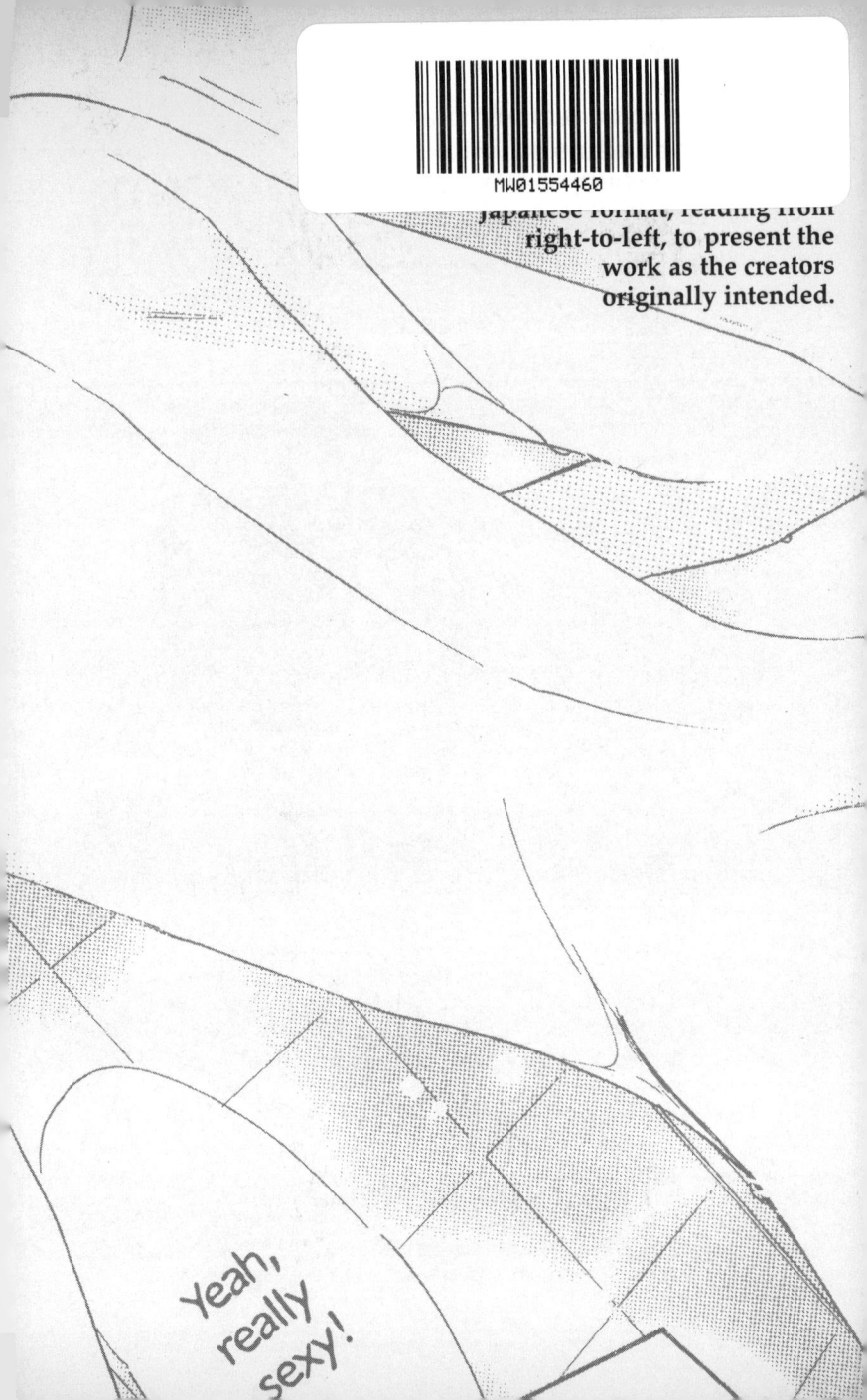

The Latest Chapter of the Most Controversial Yaoi Saga of all time!

FINDER SERIES 3: ONE WING IN THE FINDER

Story & Art by Ayano Yamane

$15.99

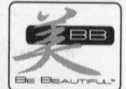

To order call: **1-800-626-4277** or visit **BeBeautifulManga.com**

Warning: This graphic novel contains violence, nudity, and sexual situations. Reader discretion advised. Be Beautiful graphic novels are absolutely not for readers under 18 years of age. All characters depicted in sexual conduct or in the nude are aged 19 years or older. No actual or identifiable minor was used in the creation of any character depicted within. Original Japanese version © 2003 Ayano Yamane. Originally published in Japan in 2003 by Biblos Co., Ltd. Be Beautiful and logo are trademarks of A18 Corporation. All rights reserved.

Delicious temptations threaten two lovers' bliss.

Selfish Love

Story and art by Naduki Koujima.

$15.99

2 Volumes Available Now!

To order, call: **1-800-626-4277** or visit **BeBeautifulManga.com**

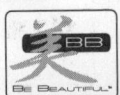

Warning: These graphic novels may contain violence, nudity, and sexual situations. Reader discretion advised. Be Beautiful graphic novels are absolutely not for readers under 18 years of age. All characters depicted in sexual conduct or in the nude are aged 19 years or older. No actual or identifiable minor was used in the creation of any character depicted within. Ad layout & copy ©2007 A18 Corporation. Original Japanese version "Kunshusama no koiha katte!" ©2001 Naduki Koujima. Originally published in Japan in 2001 by BIBLOS Co., Ltd. English translation rights arranged through TRANNET. Be Beautiful, Original Yaoi and logos are trademarks of A18 Corporation. All rights reserved.

The World's Most Famous Yaoi Epic is Back...and Better Than Ever!

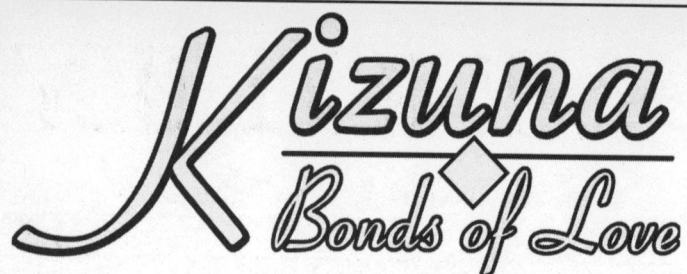

Story & Art by
KAZUMA KODAKA

"There is no better Yaoi manga"
-BoysOnBoysOnFilm.com

"I absolutely adore the artistic style of Kazuma Kodaka"
-ListerX.com

"I'd recommend this to many of my female friends"
-HentaiNeko.com

"A fantastic read"
-SequentialTart.com

"A romantic epic"
-*The Village Voice*

8 Volumes Available Now!

To order, call **1-800-626-4277** or visit **BeBeautifulManga.com**

Warning: These graphic novels may contain violence, nudity, and sexual situations. Reader discretion advised. Be Beautiful graphic novels are absolutely not for readers under 18 years of age. All characters depicted in sexual conduct or in the nude are aged 19 years or older. No actual or identifiable minor was used in the creation of any character depicted herein. Ad layout & copy ©2005 A18 Corporation. "Kizuna Vol. 7" © 2000 Kazuma Kodaka. Originally published in Japan in 2000 by BIBLOS Co., Ltd. Be Beautiful and logo are trademarks of A18 Corporation. All rights reserved.

With This Gambler, Love is in the Cards...

CASINO LILY

An All-New Romance by **YOUKA NITTA**, *the Creator of* **EMBRACING LOVE**

$15.99

To order call: **1-800-626-4277** or visit **BeBeautifulManga.com**

Warning: This graphic novel may contain violence, nudity, and sexual situations. Reader discretion advised. Be Beautiful graphic novels are absolutely not for readers under 18 years of age. All characters depicted in sexual conduct or in the nude are aged 19 years or older. No actual or identifiable minor was used in the creation of any character depicted herein. Original Japanese version "Casino Lily" © 2002 Youka Nitta. Originally published in Japan in 2002 by Biblos Co., Ltd. Be Beautiful and logo are trademarks of A18 Corporation. All rights reserved.

Enter The Garden of Unearthly Delights

VIRGIN SOIL

Story & Art by Haruka Minami

$15.99

To order call: **1-800-626-4277** or visit **BeBeautifulManga.com**

Warning: This graphic novel may contain violence, nudity, and sexual situations. Reader discretion advised. Be Beautiful graphic novels are absolutely not for readers under 18 years of age. All characters depicted in sexual conduct or in the nude are aged 19 years or older. No actual or identifiable minor was used in the creation of any character depicted herein. Original Japanese version © 2005 Haruka Minami. Originally published in Japan in 2005 by Biblos Co., Ltd. Be Beautiful and logo are trademarks of A18 Corporation. All rights reserved.

PLAY BOY BLUES

Story & Art by
SHIUKO KANO

"The Hot, Hot, HOT
Scenes in This Steamy
Manga are Reason Alone
to Buy This Yaoi"
  -SequentialTart.com

Available Now!
$15.99

To order call: **1-800-626-4277** or visit **BeBeautifulManga.com**

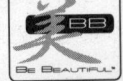

Warning: This graphic novel contains violence, nudity, and sexual situations. Reader discretion advised. Be Beautiful graphic novels are absolutely not for readers under 18 years of age. All characters depicted in sexual conduct or in the nude are aged 19 years or older. No actual or identifiable minor was used in the creation of any character depicted within. Original Japanese version "Play Boy Blues" © 2003 Shiuko Kano. Originally published in 2003 by BIBLOS Co., Ltd. Be Beautiful and logo are trademarks of A18 Corporation. All rights reserved.

An All-New Romance by **YOUKA NITTA**, *the Creator of* **EMBRACING LOVE**

SOUND OF
MY VOICE

$15.99

To order call: **1-800-626-4277** or visit **BeBeautifulManga.com**

Warning: This graphic novel may contain violence, nudity, and sexual situations. Reader discretion advised. Be Beautiful graphic novels are absolutely not for readers under 18 years of age. All characters depicted in sexual conduct or in the nude are aged 19 years or older. No actual or identifiable minor was used in the creation of any character depicted herein. Original Japanese version "Boku no koe 1" © 2004 Youka Nitta. Originally published in Japan in 2004 by BIBLOS Co., Ltd. Be Beautiful, Original Yaoi and logos are trademarks of A18 Corporation. All rights reserved.

~Haru wo Daiteita~
Embracing Love

The Ultimate Romance by YOUKA NITTA
Six Volumes Available Now

$15.99

To order call: **1-800-626-4277** or visit **BeBeautifulManga.com**

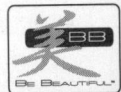

Warning: These graphic novels may contain violence, nudity, and sexual situations. Reader discretion advised. Be Beautiful graphic novels are absolutely not for readers under 18 years of age. All characters depicted in sexual conduct or in the nude are aged 19 years or older. No actual or identifiable minor was used in the creation of any character depicted herein. Original Japanese version "Haru wo daiteita Volume 5" © 2001 Youka Nitta. Originally published in Japan in 2001 by Biblos Co., Ltd. Be Beautiful and logo are trademarks of A18 Corporation. All rights reserved.

"Will leave you squirming in your seat" -*DVDVisionJapan.com*

Golden Cain

Story & Art by
You Asagiri

$15.99

To order call: **1-800-626-4277** or visit **BeBeautifulManga.com**

Warning: This graphic novel contains violence, nudity, and sexual situations. Reader discretion advised. Be Beautiful graphic novels are absolutely not for readers under 18 years of age. All characters depicted in sexual conduct or in the nude are aged 19 years or older. No actual or identifiable minor was used in the creation of any character depicted within. Original Japanese version ©2003 You Asagiri. Originally published in Japan in 2003 by BIBLOS Co., Ltd. English translation rights arranged through TRANNET. Be Beautiful and logo are trademarks of A18 Corporation. All rights reserved.

The Long-Awaited Historical Epic from the Creator of
KIZUNA - BONDS OF LOVE

MIDARESOMENISHI

A LEGEND OF

SAMURAI LOVE

Story & Art by
KAZUMA KODAKA

$15.99

To order call: **1-800-626-4277** or visit **BeBeautifulManga.com**

Warning: This graphic novel may contain violence, nudity, and sexual situations. Reader discretion advised. Be Beautiful graphic novels are absolutely not for readers under 18 years of age. All characters depicted in sexual conduct or in the nude are aged 19 years or older. No actual or identifiable minor was used in the creation of any character depicted herein. Original Japanese version ©1999 Kazuma Kodaka. Originally published in Japan in 1999 by Take Shobo Co., Ltd. Be Beautiful and logo are trademarks of A18 Corporation.
All rights reserved.

Arakawa & Izumi

Hey...
This is it for us?
I feel inferior...
There, there.
Sorry you two...
This vas the best I ould do...

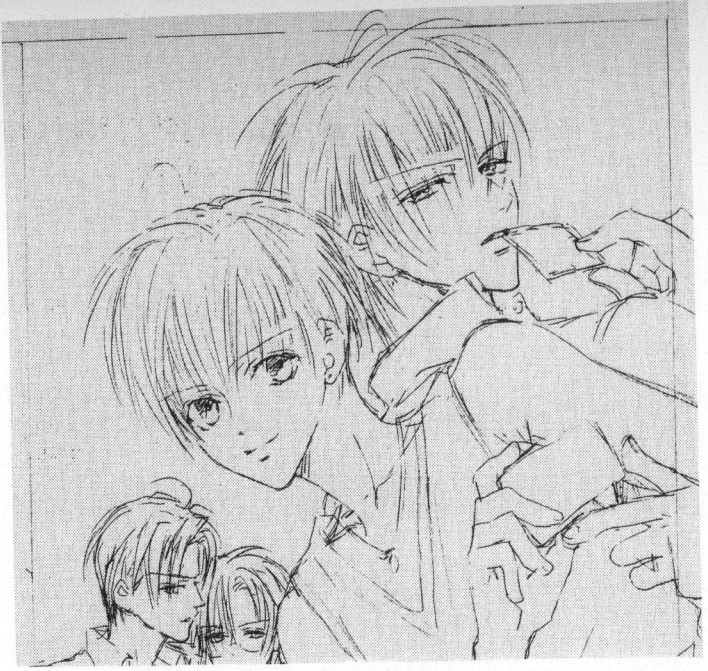

Hello! Minami here.

I wanted to change the image of this book, so the cover is rather light-hearted. As a matter of fact, it's the first light-hearted title I've ever done! The story is very comedic, but with lots of erotic scenes (LOL).

I love writing these types of stories and want to keep writing them! If I wrote erotic scenes without constraints, I can probably go 100 pages or more, but unfortunately I always have to limit the number of pages (Wah!).

Thank you to "S" my comics editor, as usual! Please forgive me for whining on the phone, and for adjusting my deadline many times when you were busy. I'm sorry. But I was able to write with all my heart. I have renewed appreciation for extra time. And to my other editor "F" - Thank you from the bottom of my heart. And my new editor "K"!! Sorry to cause problems from the start. I appreciate your continued support. And to everyone who helps me - a big thank you. And to my readers - I'm always encouraged by you. (Thank you for the letters!) I hope to see you again.

Haruka Minami

After Summer Camp

Hey Everyone!
じゃーん
LOOK!
Enough for everyone!
I made a special photo album of pictures from summer camp!
Whoa!
Wow! It's very well-made!
wow
wow
Whoa!
Really? Taishi made this?
Let's see...
open
....
No one is allowed to look inside!!
What's in it?
K... Kei, it was on a whim!
WHACK
Don't make such things on a whim!
WHACK
WHACK
I'll punch you if you look inside!!

Photos by Okunuki (LOL)

So what sort of pictures are they?
Tell me!
Well...
They're of me and Izumi...
OPEN
See?
Pictures from summer camp!
Hey Yuuri, I'm done reading this!
......。
Aside from showing him the pictures, if Izumi found out that...
I'm carrying these pictures around, he'll beat the crap out of me...
Photography Club is peaceful today.
OPEN
Erotic pictures after page two.
The End

HA
SMACK
SMACK
SMACK
SMACK
Ah... I'm...
TWITCH
Ah...
Shino'oka...! Aaahhh!
SPURT
SPURT
HA
DAYDREAMING
Then, Izumi quieted down and I...
Hey.
Are you listening to me?
Then, I made him get on top of me and I humped him...
Mm... Mmm...
CLICK
Haa...
Ah...
Ha
Ah...
Ah...
Shino-oka...
Then, I put it in from the back several times and took pictures with it in...
↑ my vision
CLICK
CLICK
That night was really good...
Hey!
Hey you!
GRIN
Shi-no-o-ka!!
SCREECH
TIP TOES ↓
Oh, sorry.
Oh...

CREAK
Ah...
PUSH
Ah...
SHOVE
Good...
More...
THRUST
SHOVE
Shino'oka is so big, and it feels so good!
CREAK
CREAK
Haa...
Mn...
Nn...
My inside's full...
Izumi... HA
SHOVE
SMACK
Ah...
Ah...
TWITCH
TWITCH
SHOVE
CREAK
PUSH
Ha...
HA
Ah...
CREAK
HA
Shino'oka...
CREAK
HA
HA

All right.
CREAK
I'll put it in...
Your perverted place...
PUSH
...Shino-oka...
HA
...Nn...
NN
HA
KISS
KISS
SLIDE
Aa... He's coming in!
SHOVE
Haa...
Hah...
A... Ah...
TWITCH
TWITCH

Shino'oka looks like he's about ready to come, too...
CLICK
CLICK
HA
GULP
CLICK
!...
HA
Hey... Shino'oka...
What?
I promise I'll do whatever you say, so...
Please, put your thing in here right now...
HA
I wanna come so bad, I'm about to go insane...
It worked!
For real?
You're really gonna let me do anything?
GRIN
HA
You can do anything...
So hurry and put it in, deep...
HA
TWITCH
TWITCH
HA
HA

BLANK STARE
Oh... Sorry...
HA
HA
It felt so good...
I forgot.
Okay, next.
It's getting even more embarrassing...
.....
HA
C... Can you see?
Spread it more with your fingers, Izumi.
But I'm so hard, I'm almost ready to come...!
SQUEEZE
Mmm...
Hurry and take it...
The sound of the shutter is like an aphrodisiac.
CLICK
Good... I can see inside.
ery nice ith the front, too.

Such an erotic sight...
Spread yourself apart wider... **Wider!**
THUMP
No way... He's looking inside there?
THUMP
SLIDE
SLIP
SLICK
Ah...
SHAKE
SHAKE
Amazing... I can see and feel you twitching.
It has such an erotic color...
CLICK
HA
BLUSH
HA
CLICK
HA
It's so embarrassing...
HA
HA
SLIDE
SLIP
PUSH
HEHE
Hey, don't squeeze my finger so tight.
You're a frisky one!
HA
I've never seen inside myself...
HA
Hah...
CLICK

No...
Ha... N...
Hah...
OOZE
SHOVE
SQUEEZE
Wh... What? Stop...
SLIDE
Ah... Nn... Hah...
CLICK
I can't spread very well with two fingers...
Hang in there, Izumi.
SPREAD
Cool air is coming inside...
JERK
Ah...
SHUDDER
HA
TREMBLE

PUSH
H... Hey... Shino...
CLICK
Ah...
SLIDE
SLIDE
CLICK
AH
CLICK
SHUDDER
Ah... Ah...
SHOVE
HA
HA
TWITCH
Ah...
SQUISH
SQUISH
SQUISH
Aaah... Go deeper next time...
Hah...
TWITCH
TWITCH
I wanna come now...
One more finger...
Ha...
SHOVE
Ah...!

HA
Like this?
HA
Is this okay?
......
Spread your legs apart more.
Your hole will be fully exposed.
Are you trying to take a picture of my anus?
Of course!
LICK
That's the best part.

HA
HA
SLICK
But we're still shooting...
Huh?
TWITCH
You'll look better with this hard and erect.
Ah...
HA
HA
HA
Huh? Ah...
SLIDE
SLIDE
I want to take more erotic pictures of you...
Roll over on your stomach.
CLICK
CLICK
CREAK
HA
He's taking pictures of me.
CLICK
Uh huh.
JIGGLE
And each time... I feel like he's conquering my body.
Nn...
This is so exciting...

Stop...!
TWITCH
His finger feels really good...
HA
はっ
TWITCH
OOZE
HEHE
The tip is soaked with pre-cum.
TWITCH
Haa... N...
Look how much your backside is aroused.
SQUEEZE
Ah...
HA
Damn... This isn't nearly enough...
Aa... More...
HA
Put your finger in deeper...
HA
HA
HA
Shino'oka, make me come... **Please!**
You want my thing in there that badly?

I feel Shino'oka's strong gaze behind the lens...
HA
HA
HA
SHIVER
SQUISH
HA
Nnnn... Ahhh.
CLICK
SQUISH
SQUISH
Ha...
Ah...
CLICK
PUSH
HE
Do you **always** put your finger in there when you do this?
HA
BLUSH
PUSH
HA
HA
No! I've never done it before!
Maybe just a little tickle around the edge!
SQUISH
CLICK
CLICK
HA
Liar... You **do** put it in, don't you?
Don't you?
Ah...
PUSH
PUSH
Ah... N...
TREMBLE

I'm so hard... So wet... It's embarrassing.
JIGGLE
Posing for Shino'oka's camera...
SHUDDER
...Is such a turn-on!
HA
SQUEEZE
HA
Take more...
CLICK
You're already so wet...
You must be really turned on.
CLICK
I can't stop my hand...
Nnnn...
SLIDE
SQUISH
N...
HA
TWITCH
CLICK
HA
SQUISH
SLIDE
It feels... Too good...
SLIDE
HA
That's hot, Izumi.
Keep **jerking it** for the camera.
CLICK
TREMBLE
HA

I might come just from taking pictures of you.
That pose is really sexy.
LICK
RISE
Shino'oka seems really excited, too.
SWALLOW
......
As long as I'm at it, I'm gonna make him grow even **bigger**.
BEEP
ZZZZZ
Okay, Izumi.
I'm taking our first erotic picture... Our remembrance.
CLICK
.....
DONE.
He... Took it...

Can I take pictures of you like this?
SMOOCH
Up close and stuff like that...
I learned about guy sex after going out with him.
HA
Hah...
SWALLOW
THROB
HA
Now... A month later... I'm out of control!
There's an intolerable yearning down there...
CREAK
HA
HA
Here.
Take it... You can do **whatever** you want.

TWITCH
...Ah...
This is a problem.
I'm starting to get shivers...
HA
Izumi.
You're erect just from my words.
Mmm...
SLIP
Pervert.
HA
Ah... Aa...
HA
HA
Who's the pervert?
HA
STROKE
SQUISH
SQUISH
STROKE
SQUISH
Ah... Shino'oka...
SQUISH

TWITCH
Mmm...
PUSH
PINCH
PINCH
LICK
Ha... Ah...
Shi... Shino'oka...
LICK
HA
ROLL
I only just touched your nipple and it got hard.
So Sexy.
It really makes me want to take your picture.
When you're reacting to me like this, I want to make it all mine.
HA
SHIVER
What should I do?
HA

B... But...
BLUS
It seems that Shino'oka has a plan...
CREAK
What are you gonna do with my nude photos?
HEHE
You're going to make me say it?
He wants to take sex photos with his digital camera.
THUMP
You know what I want...
KISS
I love you, Izumi.
PINCH
Ah...
TWITCH
SQUEEZE

ボヮーン…
FAR AWAY LOOK
What? What?
......
5 days ago...
I won't show it to anyone.
I promise, Izumi.
No.
I don't want to.
507 篠岡
Shino'oka

Hey Shino'oka. ♡
Could I see that?
CURIOUS
SHUT
Izumi Photo Album 3
泉水フォトアルバム③
You mean this?
You're always looking at those albums lately.
With the window to your back.
没頭
ENGROSSED
泉水フォトアルバム②
I really wanna know what's in it.
STARE
Which photos of Izumi are in there?
And how many volumes are there?
—...
This is...

CHATTER
Shougo, let me see that.
わははー
Hahahaha.
IMPATIENT
I haven't finished reading, Yuuri. Just wait.
Photography Club
CHATTER
Love a la Carte!
レンアイ・アラカルト!
Conscious
Mi×編
Damn!
No fun.
Calm down.
♪
STARE
Izumi Photo Album 3
泉水フォトアルバム ③

But to tell you the truth...
I got scared because I **didn't mind** 'paying' you with my body.
Huh?
I... Like **you** now.
ぽろ
TEARS
ぽろ
TEARS
When did I become like this?
I'm glad...
You weren't thinking of me as a sex outlet.
Not Takada.
When did Asakawa completely take me?
Could you **please** go out with me?
ガばっ
Whaa!
I love you, Arizumi!!
Gasp!
But I guess it's okay.
Because...
Asakawa's all mine now.

Secret Desire Beneath the Uniform • End

What?
I might as well tell you.
I've been admiring you for a long time.
I took advantage of you after finding your weak spot.
I wanted to get involved with you no matter what.
So I never had any intention of telling anyone.
I didn't realize at all...
I gave those conditions for my own convenience.
I can't believe Asakawa thought about me that way.
GRASP
I'm really sorry. When you like Takada...
......
I guess that means we're even.
Umm... Yeah.
I'm your weak spot, so I don't need to make you keep quiet.
Uhh... Yeah.
To be honest...
I was trying to find *your* weak spot so I could get out of this relationship.
......

KISS
HA
......
Why did you kiss me?
Because I wanted to kiss you.
I'm just your outlet for sex, aren't I?
So why would you kiss me?
You dummy.
I don't get hard for just anyone.
HUG
I want to touch you every day...
Because I like you.

HA
Ah... NO.
THRUST
Don't come inside me again!
PUSH
SLAP
HA
HA
Sorry...
I can't stop.
SHOVE
A...
Aaaah!
SPURT
THROB
His hot come was shot inside me so many times, I lost count after a while.
HA
HA
By the end, I didn't care about finding his weak point.
.....
HA
And I was confused by my own feelings.
HA

PINCH
Nnr
Ah
Do you realize how much you turn me on?
.....
N... Not so hard, Asakawa...
TWITCH
I'm not using a condom...
Ah...
He usually teases me during the sex.
But just now, Asakawa seemed really serious, no room for joking.
THRUST
CREAK
A...
PUSH
SLAP
CREAK
No... Ah...
CREAK
Hah...
ha
SLAP
He desired my entire body... And all I could do was squeeze him inside me.
ha
THRUST

Is there anything bad around?
Maybe he's got some incriminating papers?
LOOKING
きょろ
Your room is really clean.
Could I look at your CD's?
You can do that stuff...
Later.
SQUEEZE
TWITCH
!!!
Ah...
No, Asakawa...
Wait...
I can't wait.
You're the one that asked to come here.
FLUSH
!

...
I didn't think you'd bring it up.
Huh?
We only have limited time here, anyway.
はっ…WHAT!?
I'm an idiot. I wanted to find out more about him...
But it sounds like I'm asking him to do more to me! ♡
Come on in.
Now I'm all alone in...
Uh huh.
SHUT
Asakawa's room...
thump
Arizumi...
Nuh... Nice room! It befits you!
I think I'll go home right away.
Can I look around??

じっ
STARE
It has to be eye for an eye!
I'll have to find his weak point.
But does he even have one?
Come to think of it, I don't know anything about him.
I'll have to collect some info about him.
Equipment Room
Ah, Asakawa.
Can you extort me somewhere **else** for a change?
Huh?
It's hard to **relax** in the equipment room.
So I was thinking maybe your dorm?
I guess that's okay.
We'll go there together later.
Uh huh.
Gee, he's so agreeable...

I'm not thinking about Takada at all lately.
I'm thinking about Asakawa all the time.
Here, eat something.
I got you a special croquette sandwich.
Thanks!
It's really good.
Glad you like it!
RUSTLE RUSTLE
Y'know...
I saw you eating it before, looking really happy.
I'll bring it again.
Somathing's not right.
...
CHOMP
......
Tamed with food?
I've got to go.
I'll take my payment tomorrow, too.
This is just hush money.
If I keep doing what he tells me, he'll not only take my body but he'll take my feelings, too!
But I can't refuse him or he'll tell about me!
Lust is danger-ous.
SQUEEZE

PANT
AAh!
Aaaaahh!
Me too, Arizumi.
It really felt good.
Why am I doing this?
ずーん…
DEPRESSED
Hey...
You like it when I do your backside, huh?
Be quiet.
RUSTLE
You like my technique?
CHUCKLE
PAT
Lean on me and rest a little.
But I can't say I dislike it because Asakawa's so nice to me.
But still, I know that I'm just a convenient sexual outlet for Asakawa.

"Come to the usual place during lunch. - Takashi"
Asakawa continued with his sexual extortion.
Today? Again?
KISS
GRIN
Equipment Room
Ah...
ah...
PANT
PANT
By the third week...
Haa...
PANT
THRUST
SHOVE
SLOP
THRUST
SHAKE
PANT
I didn't have very much resistance left.
Ah...I'm coming!
THRUST

Wuh...
What if I say no?
I'll tell right away.
GRIN
I fought him for a while but there was nothing else I could do.
WRIGGLE
WRIGGLE
WHACK
LEAN
THRUST
...Ah...
THRUST
No...
And that day...
PUSH
THRUST
WHACK
Hah...
A... Ah....
Asakawa extorted the full course from me.
Ah... Nahh!
SPURT
BRR...
Since then, every day...

Mmm! Yes...
PANT
Good work, Arizumi.
SUCK
TWICH
Nnn...
LICK
Mm m..
Asakawa's about to come...
Wait...
That's enough. Let go.
?!
..... Ha...
POP
??
PANT
PANT
Asakawa? Why?
You were ready to come.
Yes, your mouth was nice.
But I want to put it in for real.
...Huh??
A...Asakawa... You don't mean all the way up my...?
Of course!

NOD
It was my 'hush money' forced by Asakawa.
STROKE
And I became engrossed in sucking him.
SUCK
LICK
SUCK
ICK
----N...
It was the first time I saw another guy's erect penis.
SUCK
...Mm mm.
The moment I put it in my mouth, I got really excited.
...Nnn.
Arizumi...
Feels really good.
Mmm...
Asakawa looks really sexy when he's excited...
SHOVE
Nnn...

FROWN
??
You thought about me that way?
Did I make him angry?
.....
Never mind.
Now... Make me come.
With your mouth, of course.
Wow!
!
.....
He's... Really big.
THUMP
THUMP
Come on, hurry.

RUSTLE
RUSTLE
Doesn't that feel good?
His light bleached hair stands out from far away.
Mmm...
TWITCH
TWITCH
M... Move your head...
He hangs out with the flashy, popular sophomores here at the college.
POKE
Hey.
I see that you're getting hard.
FLUSH
Why is he asking for my 'body'?
I've seen him around the campus but I've barely spoken with him.
Huh?
Your body **likes** kinky things.
You always seem so pure, with no interest in sex.
You knew who I am?
Of course! I've seen you around campus.
むく
LOOK UP
No, I mean, I'm not popular...
So I didn't think you'd noticed me.

SHUDDER
Ah.
Hah...
Ahh!
JERK
TRICKLE
SWALLOW
I came so fast!
FLUSH
PANT
PANT
Asakawa is used to doing things like this with a guy.
Huh...
Your voice gets raspy when you come.
I like that!
Wa!
Move your hair - it's tickly...
Why? Does it turn you on?
TWITCH

And if you refuse me, I'll tell him right away.
Oh, okay.
I had no option to refuse.
And this tyrannical bully forced me to perform sexual acts right there in the supply room.
TWITCH
き…キチク…？
Bully?
PANT
...Ah...
Hah
PANT
LICK
SUCK
ビクッ
TWITCH
ビクッ
JERK
Stop...!
I'm gonna come...!
PANT
ビクン
LICK
NIBBLE
PANT
SMACK
LICK
BITE
AH!
ゾクッ
SHUDDER

GRIN
ぐっ…
Yeah, something like that.
How much...?
Money?
I don't want that.
Pay me with your body.
Okay?
Huh?
UNTIE
HUH?
Did he just say something outrageous?
I'll take it now.
SNAP
SNAP
W... Wait...
Asakawa, I'm...
PULL
Just let me...

TAP
Wait...
What are you doing?
CHUCKLE
Does this mean...
I know your **weakness**?
If you don't want Takada to find out...
You'll have to **silence me.**
......
Could this be...
Ex... Extortion?

Out of all people, why did Asakawa have to see me?
So, you like Takada?
SHUT
This is terrible! I have to come up with an excuse!!
THUMP
I guess you like smart and serious types?
THUMP
HOLDING TIGHTLY
しっかり。
...Uh.
What am I gonna say?!
Waaah!
Sniffing dirty gym clothes, huh?
You like stuff like that?
FLUSH
No!
I don't like that stuff at all!
LIFT
HIDE
...Ah...

!?
JUMP
ビクーッ
CHUCKLE
I'm sorta surprised.
H... He saw me!
I had no idea...
That he was right outside the door.
...Uh...
You look so straight.
But you have a dirty streak.
制服の下の密やかな欲望

.....
I'll sneak a peek inside.
I became very brazen, thinking I was the only one in the room.
I opened the locker of the guy I was attracted to.
CLICK
MESSY
Takada left his gym clothes here.
He must be lazy.
THUMP
I knew it was wrong, but I couldn't help myself.
SNIFF
Oh no, I'm starting to get aroused...
It smells like Takada, his sweat, and a little detergent.
THUMP
J... Just a little whiff!
Hmmm...
Arizumi's that kind of guy.
But...
DREAMY

2 - E
It started in an empty supply room after club activities.
I forgot my book....
CLUNK
It's a hassle, but I really need it for tonight's assignment.
CREAK
SECRET DESIRE
BENEATH THE UNIFORM
制服の下の密やかな欲望
Go Takada
英和辞典
English-Japanese Dictionary

レンアイ・アラカルト!
レンアイ・アラカルト!

TURN
モグ モグ
CHOMP CHOMP
Uhh... Could I use some of our dues for this?
アッサリ.
IMMEDIATE
NO!
泉水フォトアルバム①
<- Izumi Photo Album 1
あさって
Don't bring your relationship troubles to the club.
Hey, Taishi?
I'm **really looking forward** to the day after tomorrow.
トホホ…
oh well
Me too!
And a new camera was added to the Photo Club thanks to Okunuki's own money.
Conscious/END

Hey, Taishi.
The day after tomorrow is my birthday.
JUMP
Uh...
NO.
SMILE
And a new digital camera isn't good enough?
Or would you prefer to reserve me for a day?
Gosh, Taishi.
You promised to do whatever I ask on my birthday.
After all, I did everything you wanted on yours.
Uh... Yeah, but...
After all you've done to me?
This is gonna cost you, Taishi.

Kei...
CREAK
I'm not gonna let you out of bed today.
Ah...
CREAK
Ah... I hope not!
Taishi!
Ah...!
CREAK
SPURT
Aaaaah!
3 Weeks Later.
写真同好会
Photography Club
Are you serious?
Fourteen hundred dollars?!!!
高っっ…
So expensive!
It's well over twenty five hundred with the lens!
And that's only for the camera body!
Get off it. It's cheap for an SLR camera.
And I really want it.

Besides...
If you keep licking me there, I'll come right away.
I want to come with you inside me...
HA
HA
Okay, Kei.
Slide it in... Quickly!
SQUISH
Mmm...
SHOVE
Ah, it's big!
TREMBLE
HA
HA
PUSH
Taishi... So big! Aaahhh...
HA
CREAK
PUSH
PUSH
PUSH
CREAK
Hah...
CREAK
Ah!

It's time, Kei. Are you ready?
SNAP
プチッ!!
Yes, Taishi.
HAA
は…
はぁっ
HAA
YES!
LICK
PUSH
HA
はっ
Feels good, Taishi.
HA
HA
はぁっ
SLURP
HA
はっ
Aa...
LICK
SQUEEZE
But...
I'm supposed to be doing everything for *you* today.

Nice.
LIFT
POP
K... Kei...
HA
What an erotic sight...
You're growing even bigger.
TREMBLE
SUCK
It's really big. Doesn't even fit in my hand.
I can't believe this big thing fits inside me...
Yum!

CHUCKLE
But that's what I promised...
To let you do anything with me for one day...
STIFF
STIFF
SHUDDER
Kei...
This is the best day ever...
You're so hard. So big!
I guess you like this, then.
Yeah...
Then, I'll do everything for you.

HA
はっ…
HA
HA
はぁっ
That tasted good.
Kei, you're the ***sexiest***.
Ahh...
HA
Having you like this is so exciting.

LIC
Kei, use your hips more...
This isn't enough for you, is it?
ギシッ
CREAK
ギシッ
CREAK
はっ
Ha
はぁっ
Ha
...Ha...
Let me drink more, Kei.
CREAK
ギシッ
CREAK
Ahh!
...Aa... Ah...
PUSH
SLIDE
SLOP
ビクンッ
SHUDDER
Ahh...
Hah... Hah...
SPURT
Aahh...

Eat me, Taishi.
Make me squirm.
KISS
LOVE
...Kei...
Ah...
Ha... Ah...
Ah... Taishi...
SLURP
LICK
TWITCH
TWITCH
SMACK
SMACK

Haa..
TWITCH
PUSH
Haa...
CREAK
I want some of that, too.
Bring it here.
So full of requests...
CREAK
HA
...Nh.
All right.

SHUDDER
Ah...
DRIZZLE
トプププッ...
FIZZ
Taishi... It's cold...
It'll get hot soon enough...
Nnn...
SLURP
KISS
SLURP
Hah...
LICK
LICK

CHUCKLE
Such a sexy sight...
POP
...N...
KISS
Nn... N...
GULP
GULP
Hah...
Tastes good.
I'd like to drink more...
GULP

...Ah.
KISS
I'm gonna spend the whole day...
Savoring every part of you.
Let's have a champagne toast.
Let me drink it from your mouth.
Okay.
ぱく.
OPEN
GULP
Nnn...

Hff!
What's with the outfit? I feel so... **dirty.**
SQUEEZE
You're supposed to do whatever I tell you, right?
Looks great on you... Very sexy.
Really?
This guy is a total pervert!
Yeah, it's great.
Makes me shiver...
POKE

Okay, then.
I'll do anything you say at the hotel the day after tomorrow.
SMILE
At any rate...
Two days later at the hotel.
Kei...
I've been waiting for this day.
CLINK
...Ah...

And in return...
Would you be willing to do anything I say on **my** birthday?
I'll think about it if you would...
I think he might say it's okay.
Of course I will.
When's his birthday anyway?
I wouldn't mind doing what he tells me to do.
Really, Taishi?
I promise, Kei.
STROKE

YES.
NO WAY.
Why? Can't you do whatever I say just for my birthday?
POUT
My body can't take a whole day of your perverted doings.
But I would love to do perverted things to you.
If you let me do this to you...
It would be the best birthday **ever**.
......

I want to reserve you for the **whole day**...
Wh... Whole day?
Yes.
KISS
I want a Kei that will do **whatever** I say for an entire day.
So, where did you make a reservation?
You're not making me pay for the hotel, are you?
.....
No problem!
I got a coupon for a **free night's stay** from Shino'oka.
Happy birthday.
Family owns a famous hotel.
Just as I suspected...
So... You want to make out with me for the whole day there?

ギクッ
JUMP
Y... Your birthday?
Yes!
.....
Have a bad feeling...
GRIN
You'll keep the night open, right?
So... I want a special birthday present.
Just from you!
Wh... What?

Not tonight.
I have things to do.
So heartless. You're my lover, too.
I can't help it. I'm busy with some other things, you know.
Then, how about the day after tomorrow?
It's my **birthday**.

HA
HA
SQUEEZE ♥
HA
Ah...
PULL
HA
Stop, Taishi...
The others will be here soon.
Okay, Kei. Sure.
We'll pick up where we left off later tonight.
くす
CHUCKLE

The Photo Club is rather small, with only six members.
KISS
Mmm...
KISS
写真同好会
Photography Club
KISS
Nn...
Preoccupied
As you might expect, when we aren't having meetings, our room often gets used for... **Other things.**
Hah...

コンシャス
Conscious
レンアイ・アラカルト!　番外編
- Love à la Carte! side story -

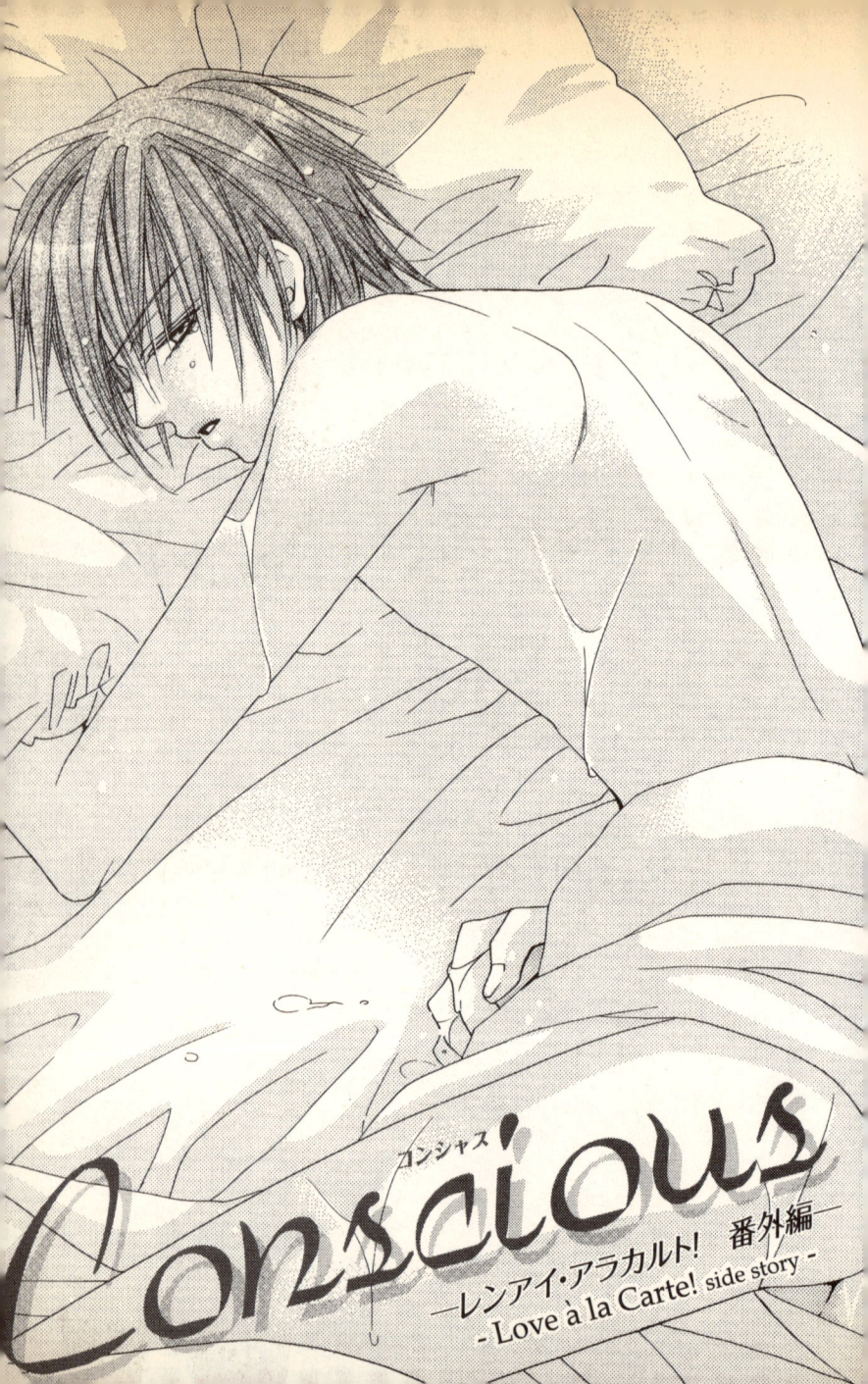

アラカル
レンアイ・アラカルト!
レンアイ・アラカルト!
レンアイ・

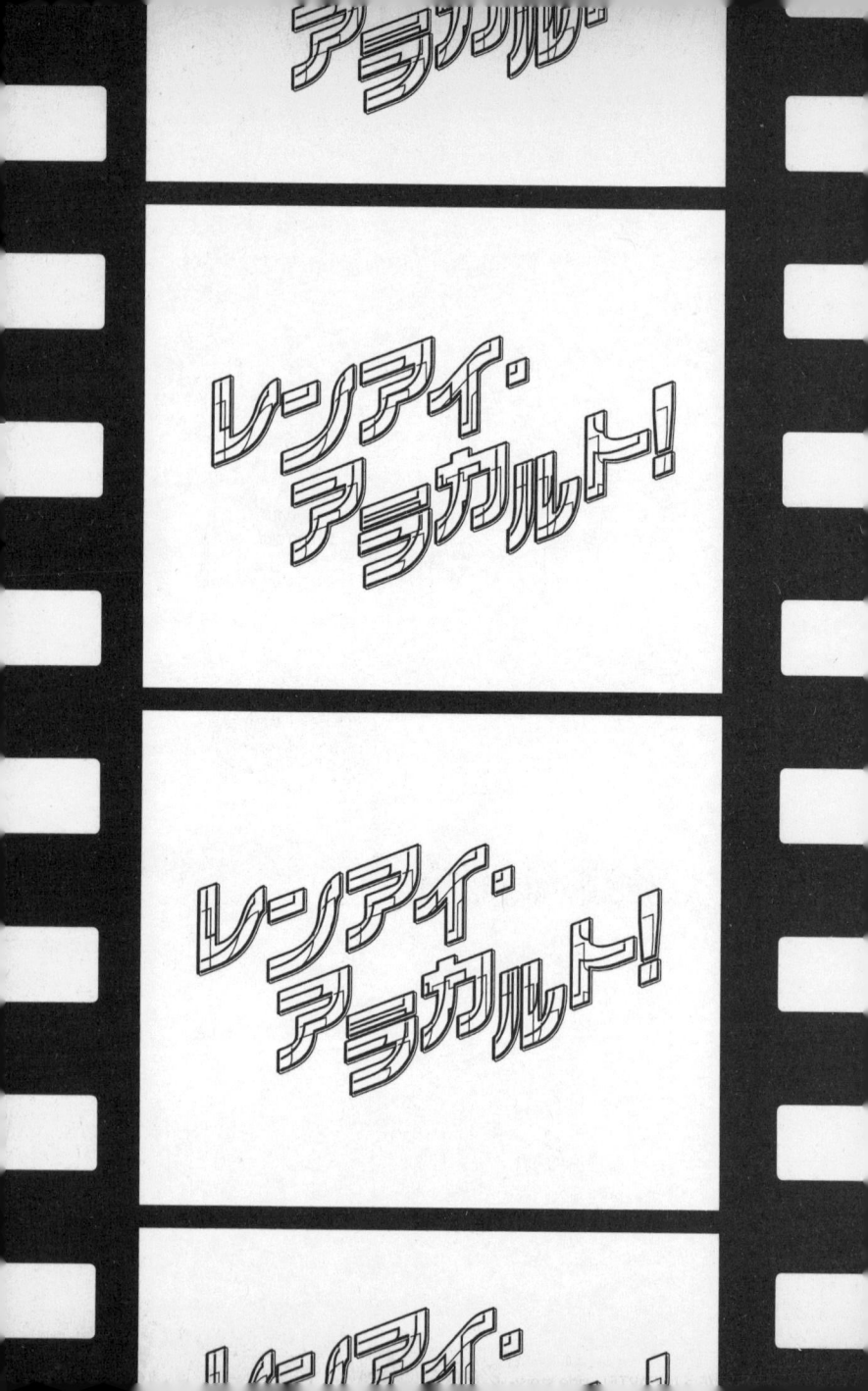

どすっ
THUMP
ZZZ
When... Did I fall asleep?
えーと。
......。
I can't remember anything after doing it with Shino'oka...
ごそ
FUMBLE
Maybe I drank too much last night?
ごそ
FUMBLE
Huh?
WHAT THE!?!?
Hmm?
ぱちっ
OPEN
WAAHHH!!!
ぶる
TREMBLE
That...
Pervert!
He noticed.
ぶる
TREMBLE
Why does he have such a thing?
Putting this on me while I was unconscious!!
It's totally see-through!
Still in their own world.
LOVE à la CARTEL side story
END

SHOVE
PUSH
Ahh...
Yes, Shino'oka... Yes!!
PUSH
Izumi...
PUSH
Ah...
Mmm...
SHAKE
SHAKE
Ah!
CHIRP
CHIRP
OPEN
I gotta go to the bathroom...
むく. UP
.....
SLEEPING

SQUISH
POP
Ah...
SQUISH
SQUISH
...Ah...
OOZE
HA
HA
Hurry, Shino'oka!
Please!
HA
I was thinking during the party...
That a drunk, red Izumi is **very sexy.**
SHIVER
Nh...
SQUISH
PUSH

Lean against the sink.
Like this?
Uh huh.
Yeah, and stick out your butt more.
Hmm?
We did it once in the shower...
But this is a first.
パチン
POP
Brought up from room
SLIDE
Nn...
Shino'oka...
SLICK

かくん
LIMP
Oops.
はっ
HA
What? You're so turned on you can't even stand?
Uh huh...
ぷるっ
JIGGLE
Hurry... Please do something about this.
HA
こすっ
RUB
Just do what I say.
DRIP
Okay.
I... Want to come.
HA
Ah...
HA

Wha...
HA
HA
TWITCH
TWITCH
Don't stop, Shino'oka... Don't stop!
SQUISH
Your underwear's getting wetter.
See... On my finger?
Your whole body is sticky.
You should take a shower... I'll wash you.
WET
Ah...
Hah...
ROLL
ROLL
My... Head's getting dizzy...
!!

Shino'oka... Stop!
TREMBLE
TREMBLE
Don't worry, I locked the door...
How is it? Does it feel good?
STROKE
STROKE
Ah...
Ahh...
SQUISH
SQUISH
POINT
HA
Shi... Shino'oka...
Feels good... More...
You're very lewd today.
Does alcohol make you more sensitive?
KISS
Ah...
How should I know?
SLIDE
!

I shouldn't have worn 'em.
Now they're ruined.
That's okay. I'm happy.
You look good in burgundy.
SQUEEZE
Ah...
RISE
Ahh... Hah...
Don't touch it so much... I'm getting all hard...
くす
I can see that it feels good.
Don't worry. I'll make you feel even better.
CHUCKLE
SQUEEZE
きゅっ
Ahh...
TWITCH TWITCH
HA

CHUCKLE
Okay, sure. I'll take it off for you.
SNAP
SNAP
Hn...
You spilled a lot... You're soaked.
SHAKE
ぺらっ…
FALL
Hah...
ZZIP
I'll bet that even your underwear must be wet.
Ah...
PULL
Izumi?
......
BLUSH
かあっ
Nice to see you're wearing the underwear I gave you.
STROKE ♥

You look drunk.
One month ago, Shino'oka and I had sex.
SLIDE
Ah...
POKE
I'll help you undress.
Hmm. I can feel your nipple.
SQUEEZE
So erotic...
Since then, I've done things like this...
Ah...
TWITCH
Hey...
Stop that and help me undress...
...With Shino'oka many times.
Ah.

Okay.
But kissing only.
Okay.
SHUT
BATH R
ふら
What a mess...
STAGGER ふら
My shirt's all wet and sticky.
もた FUMBLE
もた FUMBLE
OPEN
I got you a change of clothes, Izumi.
Hey, you didn't even get your shirt off?
Oh, Shino'oka...
I'm... I'm taking it off...!
VACANT STARE

Shino'oka seems ready to do it.
STAGGER
ふらふら
STARE
じ
ニヤッ!
GRIN
Hey, Toshiki and Yuuri!
Could you make a food run?
We're starting to run low.
Club dues
CHOMP CHOMP
もぐ
もぐ
あたりめ
Okay, get whatever you want.
We can pick whatever we want?
SMILE
SMILE
Okay! We're going!
Let's get ice cream~
CLICK
SLAM
.....
Well...
Now that we're alone, let's celebrate... Just the two of us.

Oh no! What a mess!
I'm all wet...
STARE
SMILE
Wha?
PULL
You can borrow my clothes.
I'm sure it doesn't feel good in wet clothing.
You know where the bathroom is. I'll meet you there.
I'll bring a change of clothes.
Uh huh.

!
どき
THUMP
かあっ
BLUSH
どきっ!
THUMP
Kinda reminds me...
Of how flushed you get when we're **doing** it...
くす
CHUCKLE
カァ~~
BLUSH
What are you saying, you idiot?
Move your hand!
ぱしゃっ!
SPLASH
Waah?!
つめたっ
cold!
ぽっ
POP
What are you doing, Shougo?
You're spilling sake on yourself.
わははは
HA HA HA
HA
あららっ

Thanks, Shino'oka...
Letting us use your family's place really saves the club a lot of money!
No problem! I have plenty of rooms.
GULP
So we're at Shino'oka's condo, where he lives by himself.
GLANCE
Are you okay?
THUMP
But I've been here before.
You're drinking at a fast pace, aren't you?
Huh?
Even your neck's all red.
STROKE
TWITCH

レンアイ・アラカルト! 番外編
other:side
Love à la Carte!
- side story -
やんや やんや
CHATTER
CHATTER
Tonight...
Hey Shougo!
You drinking, too?
Yeah.
There's more.
ウィ～
HICCUP
It's a party, isn't it?
I'm Shougo Izumi. The photo club I belong to is having a rowdy party.
Once again!
Congratulations to Kobayakawa!!
You're amazing!
ヒュー ヒュー
WHISTLE
わ～っ
WAAA
パチパチ
CLAP CLAP
Why? Because Kobayakawa's photo from summer camp won a National award!
Thank you.

レンアイ・アラカルト!
レンアイ・アラカルト!

That's right, Okunuki.
何かあったぞ～～な フンイキ～～
Seems like something happened ~
My... Butt...
THROB ズキ
THROB ズキ
べた～～っ
CLOSE
Good morning...
.....
He's fast!
What did they do last night?
SMILE
THUMP どき
I'm not used to him being expressive.
The two-week camp had just started.
Hey, Shougo.
Wanna go mountain biking today?
Let's go~
What?!
Bike?
NO! No way!
Let's do something else...
Why?
I wonder what kind of photos are going to be in our album?
LOVE à la CARTE! END

かぁ～
R-E-D
.....
GRIN
Huh!?
どきっ!
THUMP!
What's with that grin?
Wh... What do you mean?
Now that you let me do it with you...
You'll let me take **other pictures** of you now, right?
Like **erotic** pictures.
Pervert...?!
What are you saying, idiot?!
He did rescue me yesterday...
For real, Izumi?
I'll take that to mean you like me.
M... Maybe...
チュ♡
KISS
...Ah.
I spoke too soon...?
Good morning, you two!
Looks like you're getting along.
SHINE
Mornin'

It never bothered me when he stared at me.
So why is my heart beating so loudly today?
.....
Well... It wasn't really forced.
Huh?
Normally, I wouldn't even want to see his face.
!!
GRAB
It was a joint effort last night.
I wouldn't let you put it in if I really didn't want you to.
But for some reason, I can't stop liking him.

Not as much as my butt!
BLUSH
Still feels like something's there...
......
Why did you do that just now?!
Well, to be honest, this wasn't the *first* time.
Huh?
I've *been* taking pictures of you, too.
...But mostly of your back.
I'm jealous of Okunuki.
R... Really?
STROKE
Sorry about last night...
Forcing you to do that...
CHUCKLE
...But you're really cute...
When you're excited.
!!
BLUSH!
Y'see, I'm really troubled.
I don't think I can give you up.

カシャッ
CLICK
カシャッ
CLICK
Hmm?
Good morning, Izumi.
はっ!
HUH?!
がばっ
JUMP
Hey! Shino'oka!
Why are you taking pictures of me sleeping?!
うっ!
OW!
ズキッ
THROB
Owie...
Are you okay, Izumi?
Your back hurt?

Hey! You were gonna stop!
You look so sexy...
Were you waiting for me?
NO!
THUD
Ah.
KISS
TWITCH
Ah.
It's been a while since I smelled you, Kei.
KISS
I love you, Kei.
SLIDE
Taishi, you jerk.
I love you, too.

THUD
Get out!
I don't want you anymore!
LIFT
Ah...
LICK
SHUDDER
...Nh!
Nh...
I'm really sorry, Kei.
I won't fool around anymore. Okay?
SLIDE
Okay.
TWITCH

What?
Came to tell me more excuses, Taishi?
Perhaps.
But I really wanted you to stop being pissed.
TWITCH
If you wanna do more than talk...
SQUEEZE
I suggest you leave right now.
SHUT
Sorry, not **this** time.
I haven't touched you in so long...
FLUSH
うあっ!

KNOCK
KNOCK
Kei?
Can I come in?
ぱさ
THUD
Sure.
Come on in.
カチャ…
CLICK
Hey.
Sorry to drop by so late.

PUSH
...Aa...
Ah!
SHUDDER
SQUISH
TWITCH
SQUISH
Ah!
GLUP
Shino'oka vigorously pumped my backside.
Ah...
PUSH
Izumi...
PUSH
Ah...
Ah...
Ah!
PUSH
It felt so good back there, I could barely remember anything towards the end.

SQUISH
SHOVE
PUSH
Ah... Ouch...
Aaah...
Hah...
HA
HA
Ha...
HA
It's... All in... **Finally!**
There's so much pressure!
No way!
Aaah!
HA
This is how Shino'oka feels?
Nh...
BLUSH
HA
Are you okay, Izumi?
HA
Uh huh...
HA
HA
THUMP

I told myself that his **taking me** like this **proved** his love for me...
Izumi...
Thinking of it that way...
...Definitely helped while he slid in and out.
SQUEEZE
Ah...
SHOVE
Nh...
は…
HA
You've got to relax, Izumi.
Don't hold your breath...
He's even bigger now...
は,
HA
はあ,
HA
SHOVE
Ahh...
Ah...
はあ
HA
Yes...
GLUP
Good, Izumi...

CREAK
I love you, Izumi...
SHOVE
PUSH
PUSH
Ahh...
Hah... Aann...
TWITCH
HA
Huh...Huh... Hurry up and finish!
Shino'oka's rock hard...
SHOVE
I don't think I can **take much more!**
HA
Nh...
THUMP
HA
He's like this because he likes me...
SQUEEZE
Izumi?
Shino'oka's ready to burst...
BLUSH
Just...
Just hurry up and finish!

haa
はぁ
I've wanted to do it with you for a long time.
ぎゅっ…
HUG
はぁ
During the day when you were in your swim pants, it was all I could think about.
This is what I mean by 'like.'
Ever since I confessed to you, I could only think about **you**. I thought I'd go crazy with lust over you.
There's no way I can think of you as a friend when that is all I can think about.
Shi... Shino'oka...
ドクン…
THUMP
Shino'oka...
I said a very insensitive thing...
THUMP
ドクン…
Nh...

ギュウ
SQUEEZE
はっ
HA
No, Shino'oka...
Don't do it! I don't wanna!
ギシ
CREAK
It's just too big!
What will everyone say back at the college?
はっ
HA
ギシッ
CREAK
はっ
HA
はあっ
HA
びくっ
JERK
Izumi...
I... I can't!
Aah!
びくんっ
JERK
I'll put it in slowly... See? It's not so bad.
Ah...
はん
Aa...
SHIVER
はあっ
No... It's hot...
You're totally filling me up!
はっ
I know.
It's because I want you so badly...
Aah...
THUMP
ドクン...

THUMP
FLUSH
Oh...
Shino'oka is so... **Big!**
He wants to put **that** in me?
Izumi...
Relax. I'm going in.
CREAK
Ah...
No...
It's too big! It's gonna hurt!
SHOVE
TWITCH
!!!

POP
Okay.
SIGH
HA
I can't believe...
Shino'oka made me come twice.
So embarrassing I could cry.
DROP
STARTLE
Waaah!
Hey! Why are you taking your clothes off?
SLIDE
Shino'oka...
STIFF

Izumi...
BLUSH
HA
...Ah...
No way...
I came so easily... I'm so ashamed!
And this time all over Shino'oka...
HA
SQUEEZE
SQUEEZE
You're really squeezing...
Like my finger's being eaten.
I never experienced anything like this in college!
Shut up!
Hurry up and move your hand!

Ah!
HA
Tell me...
How do you like the feeling of me inside you?
SQUISH
SQUISH
SLIDE
HA
Ah... N...
It feels... Funny...
HA
Funny? How?
HA
I... Don't know...
SHOVE
Ah...
Ahh--!
SHUDDER
SQUIRT
SQUIRT

I've been wanting to get inside you...
HA
Wondering how it would feel...
Over and over in my head...
THUMP
BLUSH
THUMP
Eek! Just as I thought!
PUSH
Ahh!
Hey! Whacha doin' with your finger?!
Don't put it in there...
Wow.
You're really hot inside...
HAA
Ahh...
I like watching you **squirm.**
SLIDE
SUCK
TWITCH
HA
Hah...
Ah...
HA
TWITCH
HA

SQUISH
TWITCH
SLICK
SLICK
SLICK
No...
Aa...
I'm... Gonna come again...
Gosh, Izumi...
You just came but you're hard again.
HA
Shut up!
It's not my fault...
HA
SLURP
HA
It's because you're doing things to me...
Ah... Aaaah!
SHUDDER
No... Shino'oka...
HA

BLUSH
HA
HA
Wha...!
You spattered it...
All over yourself.
SLIDE
HA
SHUDDER
AH!
HA
SQUISH
SLICK
SQUISH
SQUISH
SHUDDER
SQUISH
Shi... Shino'oka...
Nice view.
Erotic from top to bottom.
That was...
HA
HAA
Don't touch me there...
SQUISH
Ah...
SQUISH
HA
Aaah!

HA
HA
I... I'm coming!!
HA
Ah!
SPURT
ビク
HA
Ah!
Aaahhh!
ビクッ
SHUDDER
I... Came so fast...!
HA
...
HA
Why?
You came really fast, Izumi.
There's lots of it, too.
HA
OOZE
TWITCH
You were so cute...
When you were coming.
HA

Ahh!
ROLL
ROLL
TREMBLE
PANT
Izumi...
PANT
Ah.
PANT
SHUDDER
No...
Ah!
PANT
SQUISH
SQUISH
SQUISH
Shino'oka's touching my thing...
Doesn't my hand feel good?
His hand is so big and hot...!
STROKE
SQUISH
SLIDE
STROKE
Don't rub me like that... Ah!
It feels too good...!!
PANT
PANT
Let go!!
A...! Aaah!
SHUDDER
SQUEEZE

...Nh.
PANT
PANT
Ah... Shino'oka!
Hah...
KISS
PANT
KISS
What am I gonna do? His touch has gotten me rock hard!
PUSH
You're getting wet down here.
Cool.
Ah...
SHIVER
Please don't touch me there...!
STROKE
SQUEEZE
Ah...!
Aaah!

FLUSH
Ah...
PANT
TWITCH
Shi... Shino'oka...
suck
Aaah...
What's wrong with me?
SHUDDER
Huh...
RUB
RUB
PANT
Please!
PANT
No, stop...
Stop!
He's sucking my nipples... And I like it!
Aren't I supposed to fight him off?
But...
Does it hurt?
You're so sensitive.
Ah...
STROKE

PANT
PANT
S...
Stop it...
CREAK
PANT
PULL
Don't take my pants off!
PANT
PULL
Don't look at that... It's embarrassing!
ズルルル...
SLIDE
PULL AWAY
PANT
Sorry.
PANT
I'm not stopping no matter what you say.
KISS
Wha...
PANT
After seeing you looking so sexy...
There's **no way** I can stop.

PANT
I'm not doing it on purpose...
You're cute, Izumi.
You're getting teary eyed.
I would've thought a college freshman like you...
PANT
It's because you're touching me with erotic hands...
You're turning all red.
SLIDE
...Would be used to doing things like this.
Is this really Shino'oka?
JIGGLE
PULL
Ah!
Wah!
かあっ
FLUSH
GRAB

RUB
SHUDDER
STIFF
Aah!
SHIVER
A...ah...
SHIVER
Stop... Don't rub me like that!
SHUDDER
SQUEEZ
Ah...
Ah...!
SQUEEZE
You're getting all hot.
I can clearly feel you through your underwear.
Huh...
You're hard...

You don't want to?
PANT
...But Izumi...
...You're getting hard.
Doesn't that mean it feels good?
TOUCH
Aa!
I see how you respond...
To my kiss... And my touch!
FLUSH
No way!
This is all a mistake!
PANIC

What's happened to my body?
KISS
SUCK
Ohhh...
Nnn...
SLICK
STROKE
...Haaa.
Ah...
PANT
ピク.
TWITCH
Shi.. Shino'oka...
Why am I getting so excited...
No...
I...
...Over Shino'oka's French kiss?

Love à la Carte!
レンアイ・アラカルト!
last-side
Final Chapter

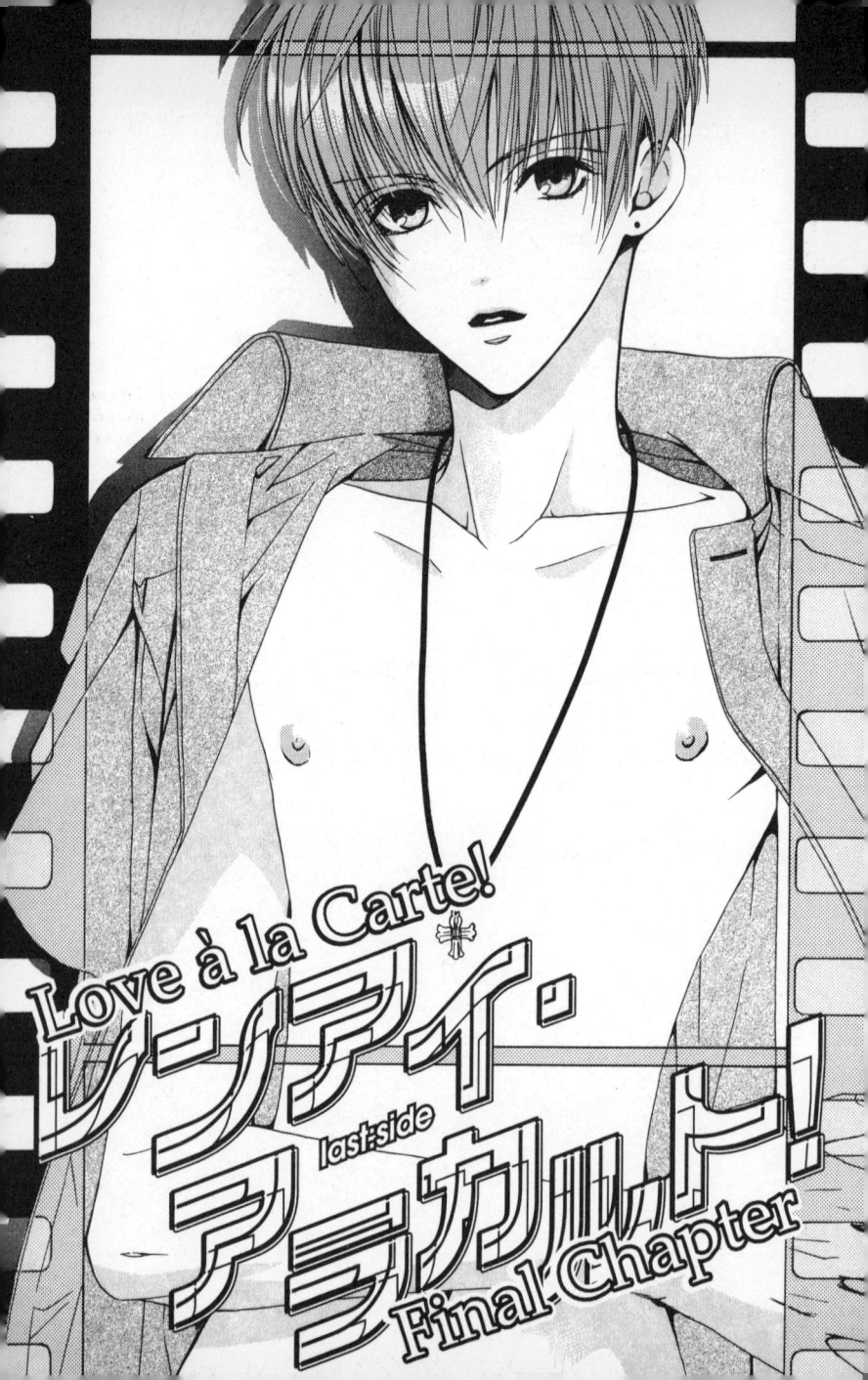

Izumi!
...
The reason my body is so hot and trembling...
Is because Shino'oka infected me with himself!
Shi... Shino'oka...
That's why...
Ahh...
I'm so excited.

SHAKE
Ah...
Shino'oka's body is really hot.
Mn...
Shi... Shino'oka?
Ah...
No, it's not just the body.
PANT
LICK
KISS
KISS
Everywhere I touch is hot...
What am I gonna do?
It's his breath, his tongue.
A... Aahh...
SHIVER
TWITCH
Hah...
SHOVE
TREMBLE

But you said you like me...
With such a cool look on your face.
Me?
Yeah.
So I couldn't tell if you were serious or not...
HUG
I was really nervous...
I had to prepare myself.
Telling a guy I like him.
I love you, Izumi.

But I don't understand!
PANT
Why are you doing this?
PANT
I just can't let **someone else** have you...
CREAK
Before I had a chance to do it with you!
GRASP
I'm not gonna just pretend to be okay!
Shino?
!!!

Huh?
You should have said...
No to me back then.
He was acting cold toward me...
Now I just can't give up on you.
And it was my fault?
Izumi?
Ah!
W...wait. Shino'oka!
Because I said that?
SHUDDER
No... Shino'oka.

This is no different from what Okunuki did!
Maybe worse!
I thought you were a nice guy!
Yeah, the same as Okunuki.
But I'm...
Sick of being a nice guy!
SQUEEZE
Last month in the club room.
I know you were trying to be polite...
But being "just friends" with you...
CREAK
Is too painful for me.
No...
And...
I have to stop the pain!

That's not what I'm asking!!
Wuh... What are you doing in my room?
What?
I came to attack you!
Izumi.
FLUSH
CREAK
No...
Stop!
Shino-oka!!
THUD
CREAK
Aaah!
...!

Huh?
CREAK
CREAK
CREAK
CREAK
CREAK
ばっ
JUMP
...?
CREAK
I'm sure I locked the door!
CREAK
CREAK
Oh?
Izumi?
Are you still awake?
?!
SURPRISE
CREAK
Shi... Shino'oka.
Wha...?
THUMP
Wasn't that door locked?
THUMP
STEP
STEP
Oh.
I have spare keys for **all** the rooms...

It fell...
It was still big, too!
DROP
.....
ポッポッ
FLUSH
ポッポッ
FLICKER
FLICKER
I wonder...
Still at it.
sigh...
I can't fall asleep.
!
モン モーン
AROUSED
I just can't stop thinking about Shino'oka. What am I gonna do?
FUMP

Come on, Suoh. You, too!
Ah...
....
FLICKER
Now that I'm aware of him, I can't help myself.
I'd better keep my guard up around him.
Uh... Thanks about before.
he he he...
Wonder if he thinks about me while masturbating...
Sure.
Am I an idiot?
Being so nervous...
FLUSH
He **did** say he likes me.
Wonder if he does...

Slapped by Kobayakawa...
Look this way! ♡
Here we go.
CLICK
CLICK
Take a good one!
He never learns...
As if nothing ever happened.
GLANCE
......
Our eyes still always meet.
Hey Shino'oka, come over here.

!...
Okunuki's bad behavior surprised me.
But Shino'oka's attitude surprised me even more!
Ah.
He saw down there.
ドキ THUMP
ドキ THUMP
Yay!!
Hahaha Yuuri.
Double fireworks!!!
SPARKLE
わはは~ HA HA HA
SPARKLE
Whoa! Watch it!
I only have a tiny sparkler.
It's gonna go out!
Hey you two!
Sorry.

BRUSH
sigh
BUMP
こつん
You're too careless!
Don't you realize how much I **worry** about you?
Huh?
He usually seems so emotionless... So indifferent.
Um...
But he got so emotional when it was about me!
Does he really like me?
TURN
ふい!
Don't be alone with him again!
Dry yourself well.

Ha...
Huh?
My legs are weak now that I'm relieved...
Ooops.
LIMP
Izumi!
Are you okay?
How embarrassing.
Sorry.
Wait a sec...
Let me get a towel!
Oh.
COVER
Th... Thanks.
......
FROWN

Taishi...
Can I have a word with you? In private?
ひややか
GLACIAL
ウッ...
GASP
....
I'm sorry, Izumi.
DEJECTED
...??
I'll tell Taishi to stop harassing you.
......
GLANCE
I'll take Taishi with me...
So take care of him, Shino'oka.
SHUT
Maybe...
Kobayakawa is the most powerful member of the club?
He sure ordered Okunuki around.
Ha haha.

Shi...
Shino'oka.
You really came...
...
Hey! You can't just barge in like this!
You must've been listening!
You're rude, Shino'oka!
Stop fooling around, Okunuki!
GRAB
SHAAA

!!
Hm?
BANG!!
Oh...

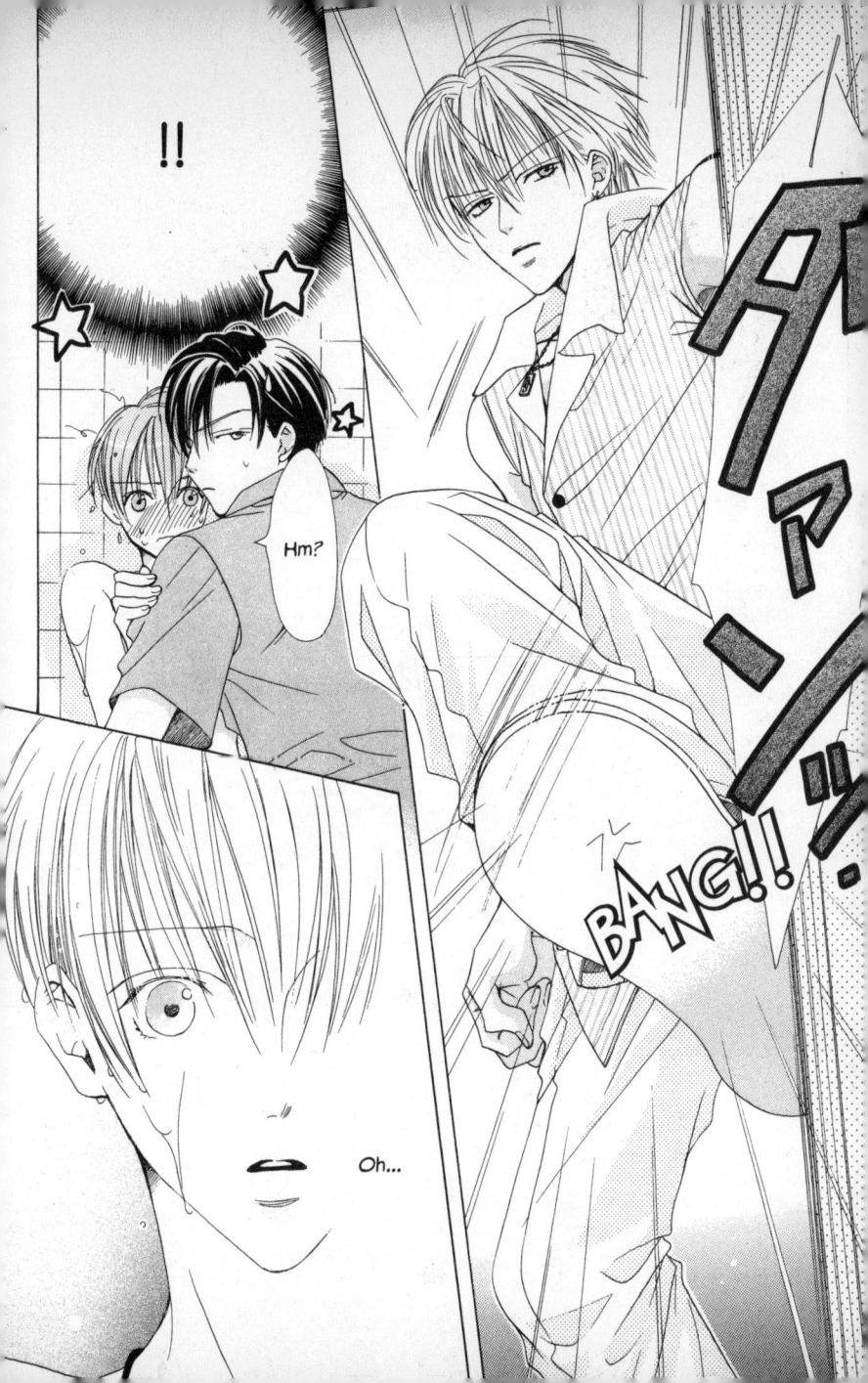

SLIDE
heh
What a sexy voice!
!!?
...!?
SHUDDER
Ah...
Please stop, Okunuki!
SHAAA
hee hee
Izumi, you're shaking.
Is it the **first time** someone's touched your backside?
...Just to have a perverted guy touch me like this!
SHUDDER
Ah.
I can't have come to summer camp...
Stop!
Okunuki!
Damn it! If you really like me, you'd come rescue me, Shino'oka!

You fit right in my hand!
Hah...
Okunuki! Stop!
Don't rub me there!
SQUEEZE
びくっ
SHUDDER
A... Ahh!
D...
LICK
びくっ
TWITCH
Nice shape, too. **Very cute!**
You'd be perfect as my model.
I really don't want to hear this!
ROLL
ROLL
Wuh...
Wait Okunuki!
Ahh...
Hah...

Ah!
LIFT
Izumi...
What am I gonna do?
じり...
CLOSER...
I'm **seriously** in trouble!
I want to photograph **all of you...**
Not just the **play pictures** I've taken so far.
Listen...
I want to know you more **deeply.**
TOUCH
Aaah!!
JUMP
Ah!

Wait...
I've been wanting to see you up close.
Okunuki...
This isn't funny...
I want to see **every** part of my cute model's body!
SHAAAA
heh
I know that.
I'm being **serious.**

Love á la Carte!
レンアイ・アラカルト!
second:side
Chapter 2

SLAM
No way!
Izumi...
SHUDDER
SHOWER
I can't let you out yet!
What? Why!
Okunuki?

Lean your hands against the wall.
Okay.
TAP
ザァァァ...
SHOWER
CLICK
Lean forward a little...
Now spread your legs and look this way!
CLICK
CLICK
Yeah, really sexy!
Umm...
Wait a sec...
CLICK
Isn't this pose a little too erotic?
Ah!
Okunuki... I really have to go!

CLICK
CLICK
Okay, look away!
uh huh.
Good, good!
CLICK
Just like that!
......
I really want the whole body...
Could I take a picture of your back?
You mean... With my **butt** showing?
uh huh. ♡
Well, it's just my butt.
DROP
Could you hurry up? I'm starting to feel like a prune.
Okay...
CLICK
Maybe a different pose!
Let's see.
CLICK

I'm so happy you're into it.
Okay, here we go. ♡
!…
But really, waist up only!
SHUT
CLICK
We'll start with an orthodox one.
Look this way!
CLICK
SHOWER
Like this?
Great! ♡
You're so sexy, Izumi!
CLICK

What?
That's crazy!
Oh, no, no!
あはは ha ha ha
Nothing pornographic!
I promise to shoot your picture from the waist up!
This is just a reminder of our stay... I want to make an album for everyone after camp!
An album? For everyone?
Uh, huh. ♡
Maybe if Shino'oka sees these pictures...
ぷくくっ SNICKER
!
His expression will finally change!
Okay then... how about a really sexy one?
THUMBS UP!
Of course! ♡

sigh...
SHOWER
I just don't get Shino'oka!
Why does he like me, anyway?
KNOCK
KNOCK
Izumi!
Hello!
Oh, Okunuki!
Why did you bring a camera to the shower?
GRIN
GRIN
Well...
I wanted to add some ***sexy scenes*** to my collection!

It's more fun with lots of people...
So why don't you join us, Shino'oka?
No, thanks.
I'll skip it.
Huh?
DING DONG
Must be the delivery!
Is he avoiding me?
It's disconcerting.
Did I hear him wrong when he said he likes me?
MUNCH もぐ
もぐ MUNCH
What's with him?...
SPATTER

Huh?
He looks surprised.
How about it?
You probably didn't **do such things** on your senior trips...
When you went to those **rich, private campuses!**
ANNOYED
What kind of campus do you think I went to?
Really?
How insulting!
Other than being expensive, it's no different from any other college.
I'm curious now.
What were you like before? I wanna know.
Why don't you join us tonight?
What? Sounds like fun!
Could I come, too, Yuuri?
Of course, Toshiki!
…!
CHATTER
CHATTER

We'll stay up all night!
He's staring at me again!
Okay.
GRIN
Wanna join us, Shino'oka?
Sort of **boring** with just the two of us!

Hmm..
I'd like to be with Shougo! ♡
Wha!
ぎゅっ.
GRAB
I want to photograph you while you're sleeping!
That shot will complete my **Shougo Photo Collection Album!**
No fair, Taishi!
You can't hog a model.
I'm gonna complete the various versions any day now. ♡
Whaddaya mean?
For real?!
There's a room for each person...
Your room number is printed on your key!
How boring - - private rooms.
Sigh!
Shougo, Can I come visit tonight?
Yeah.
Let's have a pillow fight! ♡

Really?
We'll do them tonight!
Definitely! Fireworks in the summer!
CLICK
—...
Which rooms are we using?
Wow! It's huge!

ジーっ
STARE
You said it, but do you really like me?
I'm right in front of you...
But your expression doesn't change.
...?
What is it, Izumi?
ha ha ha
Ah... It's nothing.
OPEN
It's awkward to ask him now...
Oh yeah... I brought some fireworks!

Here.
Use my towel.
Uh...
Thanks!
WIPE
ふき
ふき
Um... Yeah.
We were thinking about getting food.
You're hungry, right?
....
"I like you"
Ahh... Shino'oka?
GRASP
I can't believe it!

It's a little early for dinner, but wanna eat now?
There's a restaurant nearby that delivers.
That sounds good.
Yeah, I'm starved!
Let's eat!
I wonder what's on their menu?
♡ Gosh, Shino'oka...
Thanks for letting us use your vacation home.
GRAB
We're not using it this year, anyway.
PUSH
SPLASH
SLIDE

I joined the photo club...
Because I like you.
Huh?
I was rather surprised by this...
But he said it with such a cool look on his face.
Ah..umm.
Really? Thanks!
We'll stay friends!
That's what I said back to him...
PULL UP
はき
And he hasn't said anything since.
はき
PULL UP

Look Shougo! ♡
Like my swim cap?
すい
GLIDE
Stop doing that!!
Give it back!
WHACK
!
Ouch
Creep!
Now's my chance!
AIM
A month ago...
I was alone in the club room with Shino'oka...
Oh no..
SPLASH
DISAPPOINTED
ぶく BUBBLE
....
BUBBLE ぶく

じっ
STARE
But Shino'oka...
He looked away again.
TURN AWAY
I can't read his expressions.
I think Shino'oka...
...Likes me.

That Shino'oka...
SPLASH
...Is staring at me again!
Suoh Shino'oka is also a college Freshman.
His family owns a famous hotel. He's rich.
He looks flashy, but he also seems distant and mysterious.
I don't talk to him much...
...But our eyes keep meeting.

Stop it!
バシャン
SPLASH
Don't do that, Yuuri!
Izumi will become Taishi's victim!
SPLASH
バシャッ
Cut it out, Takagi!
TUG
No way! ♡
I got you now! ♡
WAVE
ぴらっ♡
Oh!
Nice, Takagi!!
See...
CLICK
Izumi, turn this way!
CLICK
Come on, give it back!
And...

SPLASH!!
WAHH!
!!
Why you... I got water in my ear!
And this energetic one is Yuuri Takagi, my buddy for the past few years.
Wow! Feels great!
Shougo, let's do that game! ♡
Huh?
This is Toshiki Fujinami, the college sophomore who keeps Takagi in line, for the most part.
What game, Yuuri?
You know the game... It's called Pull the Pants Down!
Didn't you play it too, Toshiki?
Oh no!
Here!!
ばしゃっ SPLASH
WAAAA!

What a great pose!
Would you let me photograph you **nude** sometime?
You have a beautiful body line.
CLICK
No way!
You'll have to settle for the swimsuit.
FLOAT
FLOAT
CLICK
This guy who keeps taking my pictures is ***Taishi Okunuki,*** *a college sophomore. He's good-looking but kind of strange.*
Yes, it's probably best to avoid **that**, Izumi.
Taishi wouldn't let you get away with **just** a nude picture!
GLANCE
He's ***Kei Kobayakawa,*** *the most intelligent of the group, and the responsible party of the bunch.*
GO!!
ばっ
JUMP!

Love à la Carte!
レンアイ・アラカルト!
first:side
Chapter 1

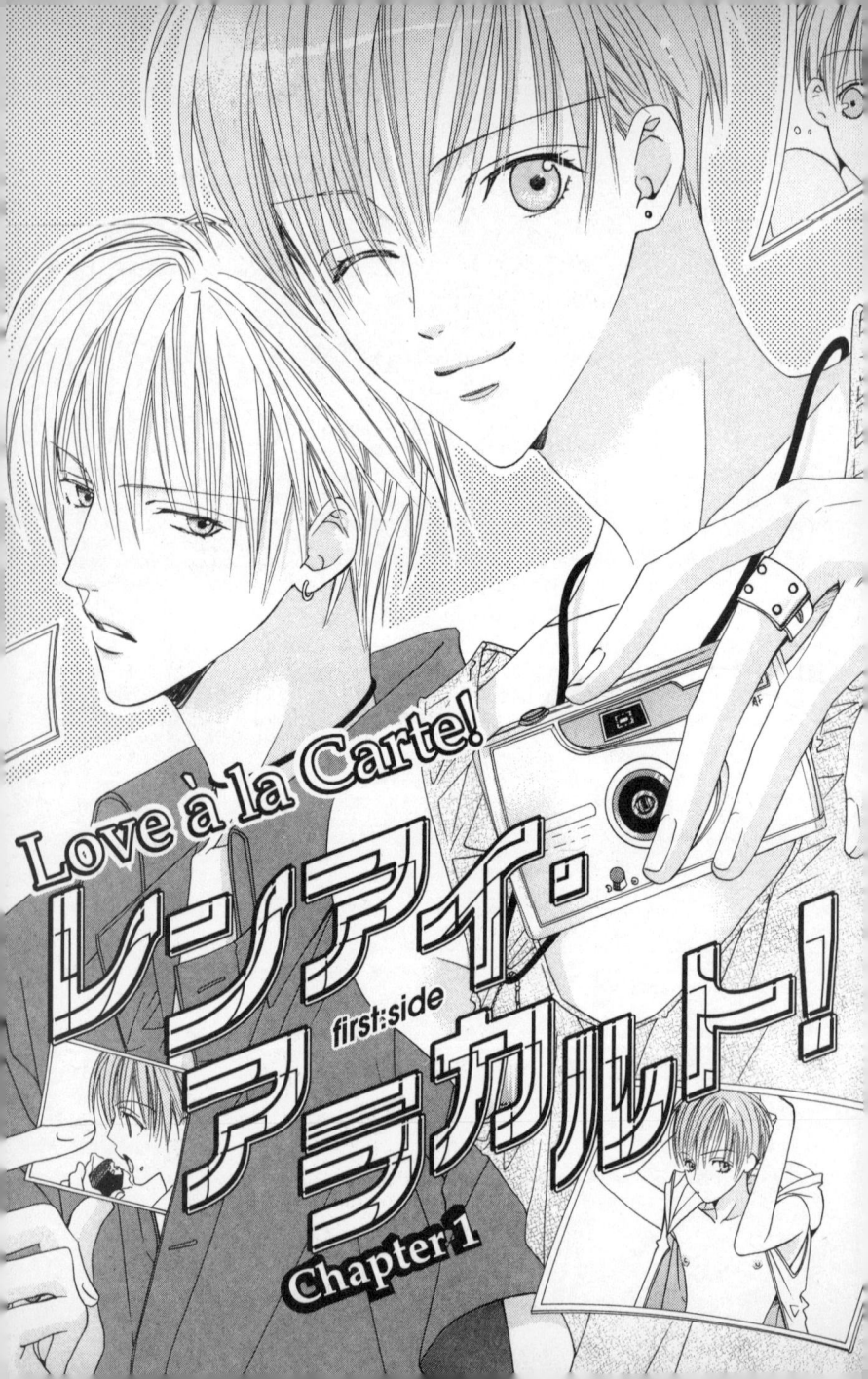

Okay, Izumi. Look this way!
CLICK
You look sexy when you're wet.
We have the best looking guys!
I wanna take some pictures too!
CLICK
This is my first summer vacation since starting college.
Why's everyone photographing me?
It's not much fun to photograph a guy... **usually.**
SPLISH
SPLISH
It's great fun!! ♡
good
I invited you here so I can take lots of pictures of YOU!
What? **Fujinami** is **much** cuter than me!
SWIM
スイー
He punches if you try anything.
I'll pass.
I hate being photographed.
SMILE
I guess it's good that I joined. ♡
♪
ぷかー
FLOAT

レンアイ・アラカルト!
first:side
Love á la Carte!
I'm Shougo Izumi.
Today's the first day of Summer Training Camp for the Photo Club I belong to.
Here we go!!
SPLAAAASH!!
SPLASH
Haaaah...
It feels great!
Pools are the best!
This is basically just an excuse to stay in a nice vacation home in Karuizawa for two weeks.

レンアイ・アラカルト!
レンアイ・アラカルト!

CHARACTER

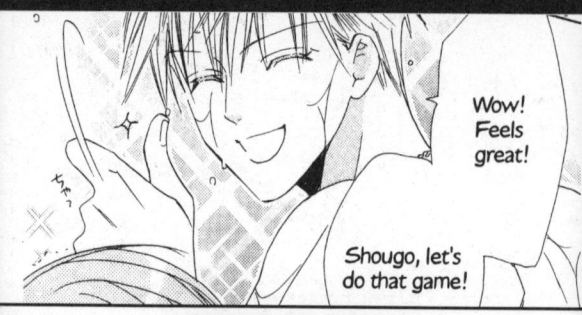

YUURI TAKAGI
Izumi's longtime friend can be brash, loud and boisterous, but he has a good heart...Except when he's playing "Pull The Pants Down" and stealing Izumi's swim trunks.

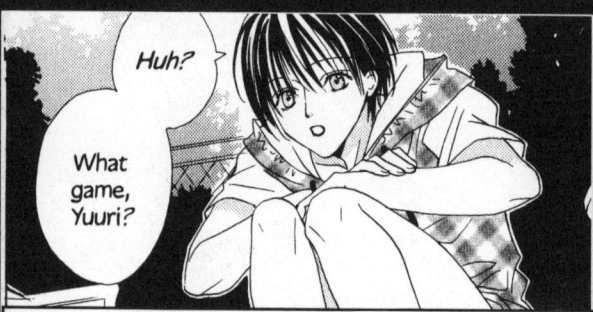

TOSHIKI FUJINAMI
This good-hearted soul keeps Takagi in line as best as possible, but it's unclear when he'll use his beautiful body to win the heart (and lusts!) of his brash friend.

PROFILES

CHARACTER

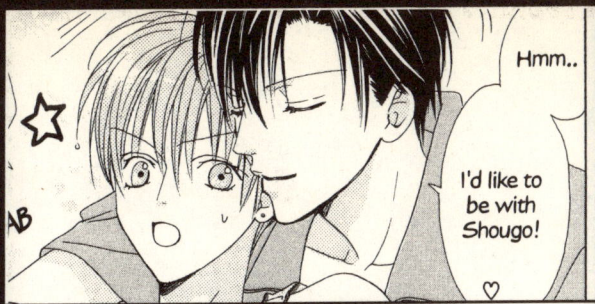

TAISHI OKUNUKI
He'd like to claim Izumi's body for some extracurricular activities, including an erotic nude photo shoot or two. He wouldn't mind claiming him as a lover, either.

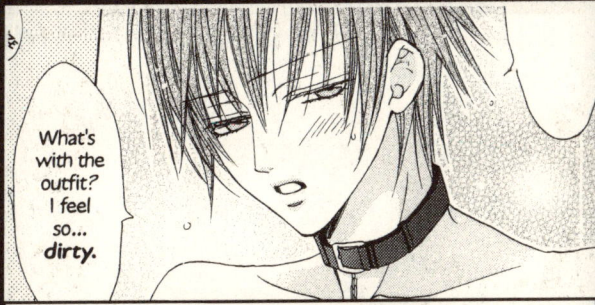

KEI KOBAYAKAWA
The intelligent member of the Photo Club has a huge crush on Taishi, and will even go so far as to forsake his usually responsible behavior to claim the charismatic photographer as his lover.

PROFILES

CHARACTER

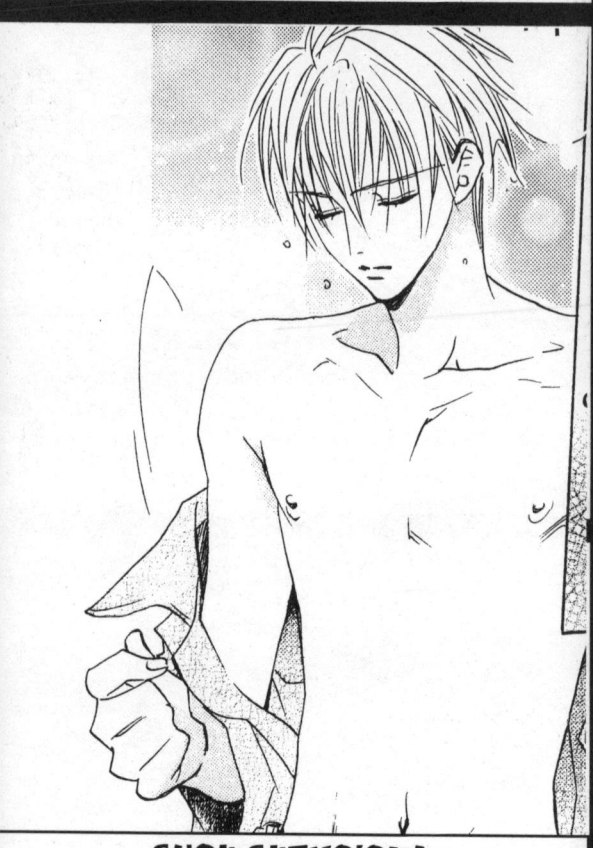

SUOH SHINO'OKA
Handsome and aloof, Shino'oka passionately craves Izumi's body. Although he comes on too strong at first, his persistance may be the thing to claim Izumi's innocence.

PROFILES

CHARACTER

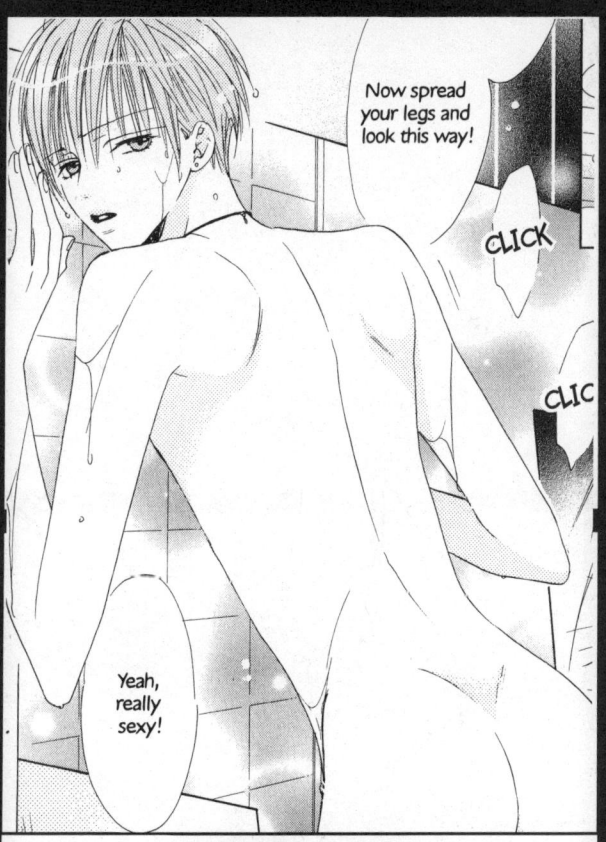

SHOUGO IZUMI
Enjoys the summer Photo Club mostly for the extended stay at a nice vacation home in the country and the easy access to the other male members. Not as innocent as he looks.

PROFILES

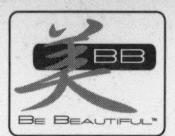

LOVE À LA CARTE

Story and Art by
Haruka Minami

Translation
Emi

Publisher
Mariko Kumanoya

BeBeautifulManga.com

Love A La Carte. Published by Be Beautiful™, an imprint of A18 Corporation. Office of Publication – 250 West 57th Street, Suite 1728, New York, NY 10107. Original Japanese version "Renai a la carte!" © 2003 Haruka Minami. Originally published in Japan in 2003 by Biblos Co., Ltd. English version © 2007 A18 Corporation. Be Beautiful, Original Yaoi and logos are trademarks of A18 Corporation. All rights reserved. Price per copy $15.99, price in Canada may vary. Printed in Canada

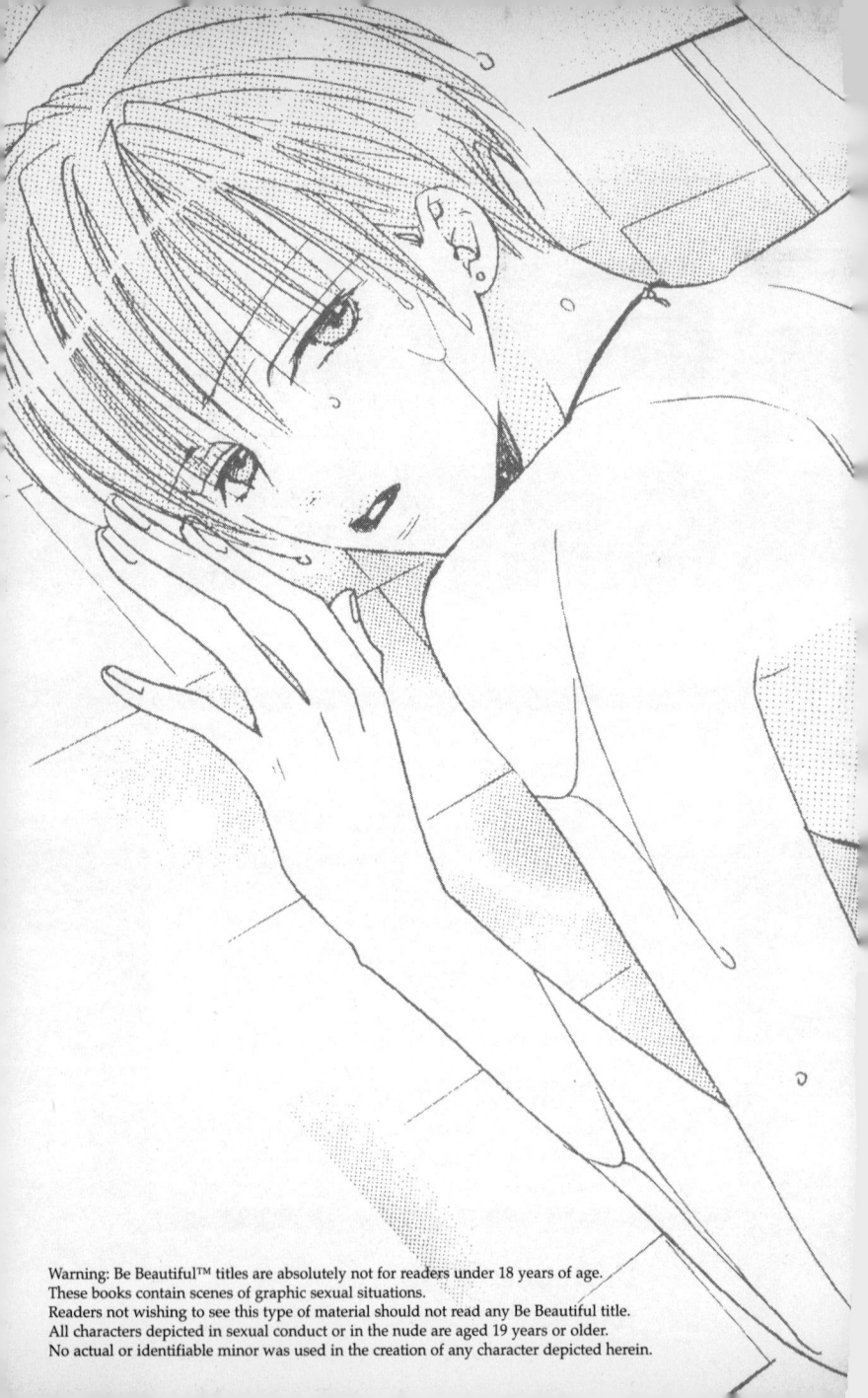

Warning: Be Beautiful™ titles are absolutely not for readers under 18 years of age.
These books contain scenes of graphic sexual situations.
Readers not wishing to see this type of material should not read any Be Beautiful title.
All characters depicted in sexual conduct or in the nude are aged 19 years or older.
No actual or identifiable minor was used in the creation of any character depicted herein.